A HOLIDAY MYSTERY

A MURDER
IN
Benidorm

Dedication Page:

I am dedicating this book to my family. Without the great family holiday we had at Benidorm, I would not have had the inspiration to write this story!
I love you all.

Copyright

Chapter 1

It was finally over. She had just typed the very last word of her manuscript. Now, she just needed to send it over to the publisher. She scratched her head and looked around, scanning her eyes over the scattered pages of her notes all over her desk, surrounding her computer. But first, she thought, she must find the address... wherever it was.

She began flipping through the notes, spreading them further along the table, reading them at a glance: Title page, character notes, throw away lines, random dialogues... and there it was, holding up the mug of coffee. She attached the document to the email and clicked send. Now, she just had to wait, which was something she was never good at. Waiting around was for people who had nothing better to do. She thought for a moment and switched on the television. Bargain in Britain lit up the screen. Forget Britain, she thought with a smile. "I'm gonna go to Benidorm."

There were a few things that she was going to have to buy before getting on the plane, and she will also need to buy a ticket. But when can she go? Will they have a spot this side of the month? She wasn't usually one for spontaneous trips and dreaded to think how much it was going to cost her to have a holiday so soon.

She picked up the phone and dialled the number for easy jet, the only line she ever used. It was cheap and easy, and her past experience with them hadn't been unpleasant. She listened as the phone began to ring on the other side.

"Hello, Easy Jet airlines, how can we help you today?"

She smiled, and pushed the phone closer to her ear. "Hello, my name is Kate and I would like to go on holiday to Benidorm please?"

"Of course, when would you like to go?"

She smiled, this was the part she was interested in. How soon can she fly? Today, tomorrow, next week? "When is your earliest availability?" she asked.

"Let me check that for you?"

There was a brief pause. She could hear the receptionist tapping away at the keyboard. The fast clicking and tapping, sounded through the phone until it paused. "Ok," she said, still holding on to the phone. "The next availability we have is next week on thursday."

"That's great. What time?" she asked. She needed to be ready.

"The plane leaves at ten, so be sure to be here early."

Kate nodded and smiled, before thanking her and hung up the phone. Next thursday. That left her with six days to prepare and then, she can relax and find some inspiration for her next book, whichever that may be.

Kate looked around, Of course, there were things she had to take care of first.

"Benidorm is going to be awesome," she thought to herself. She looked through the photos and tried to decide where to stay. Hotels were pretty good, and there was one right by a robin hood resort. "Classic," she commented. And the area wasn't bad either. She booked the hotel nearest to the resort, and paid. Now, all she had to do was go shopping.

She grabbed the largest bag she owned and grabbed her purse. It was time to go shopping for some more clothes.

Kate's head hurt the moment she went into town. There were too many people, too many lights and too much noise. She grit her teeth together, and hastily made her way into the first store, where she hoped it would be quieter.

The airport was crowded and loud, worse than it was in the town centre. Everyone crammed together, trying to get a seat in the waiting area. Even the coffee bar was full. She welcomed the familiar scent and went to grab herself a cup. She glanced down at the time. It was five in the morning. She had five hours before the plane was due to take off, which meant she had an hour before she needed to be booked in. Not wanting to wait, she made her way to the front desk and showed the ticket. Then, she was led to the luggage department. Her small bag, filled with clothes and her writing equipment, sat on the scales. She thought for a moment, then asked them if she could take it on the plane with her—she hoped she could write on the way, or at least get an outline written for when she landed.

They agreed and then pointed to the belt, where everything got scanned. Which meant, taking the laptop out of its case. An annoyance, but she did it and waited on the other side. She flicked her long hair behind her ears and pulled out her earrings, placing it on the tray, along with her keys. Thankfully, she didn't have to wait long and collected her things on the other side. She was the first one in the line to board. She smiled again to herself, so far, this was a breeze. She'd heard horror stories of being pulled up and denied the flight, though she had never experienced it herself, though a few people were subjected to a drug test. Rumours were, aids were pulled apart to smuggle in some substances. Idiots. She boarded the plane and took her seat by the window. She let out a sigh and studied her reflection. Her hair was all over the place, putting the 'messy' in 'messy bun'. The hair pins she used barely held the bun in place. Her bronze eye shadow, thankfully, held its colour, and she had managed to keep her clothes clean; compared to her usual clumsiness and coffee stained shirt.

A couple sat behind her, pushing against the chairs as they squeezed into their seats.

"I can't believe you!" a woman gasped, snarling.

"It's not my fault!" her partner snapped back. "I said 'first class'. I didn't know that it was going to be so busy."

Kate turned her head, slightly to peer over her shoulder, watching the reflection of the couple fighting. She rolled her eyes and pulled out her laptop. Now, what was going to be her next story? Her first book, A Shortcut to Heaven was a mystery. She thought for a moment. Mysteries were popular. She smiled. Perhaps, writing a mystery series would be fun.

She opened a new document, and began to plan out her new story. If she could get the outline done before she landed, then she'd be able to write as soon as she found a nice spot to sit in.

The plane landed, and she closed her laptop. She placed it back into her bag, still pondering on the story. She had it outlined to some extent. She knew the characters name, locations the story was going to be set in, mapped out the route, and she knew what the stakes were going to be. Everything she needed to start with, she had prepared. She stood from her seat and followed the queue off the plane and into the Spanish airport. The heat immediately greeted her with a blinding light of the sun.

She hailed a taxi and made her way to the hotel, excited that her holiday was finally getting started.

The hotel stood on the corner of a road, right in front of a roundabout. The roads were narrow, but the traffic was slower than what she was used to. The Hotel's entrance swung open, with its double doors open on both sides. She stepped in, passing the white painted walls, which smelled like fresh paint. Inside, the floor gleamed in the sun, reflecting the glitter mixed in with the marbled flooring.

"Hello," Kate said, stepping to the front desk. "I booked a hotel room. Is it ready yet?"

"What's your name?"

"Kate Monty," she replied, smiling.

The receptionist typed into the computer. "Yes, your room is ready." She grabbed the key from behind her, and then pointed to the stairs as she handed it to her.

"The second floor, second door on your left. Number eighteen."

Katie thanked her, and headed for the stairs. She frowned. The stairs were narrow and steep. It followed up the curve of the building, with the rails framing either side of the staircase.

Her hotel room's door was painted black. The number one was tilted to one side.

She slipped the key over the sensor and then pushed the door open. The door led to the living that overlooked a small balcony, with double glazed windows. She took off her shoes, feeling the smooth hard surface of the laminate flooring.

The cold air blew against her, the moment she stepped through the doorway, greeting her like a friend. She breathed a sigh of relief, and then made her way to the windows. Her view from the balcony overlooked the resort's pool and jacuzzi. "Beautiful," she gasped. No doubt, she would enjoy the water later. But first on her agenda was to find a spot she can write in—one away from distractions, but some place she could still enjoy the view of what Benidorm has to offer.

She found herself sitting at a small table, between the bar and the ocean. The cool sea breeze, as little as it was, came as a welcome to break up the intensity of the summer blaze. The table came with a canopy, shielding the computer, and herself, from the glaze. And, she could see some of the screen.

She glanced at the outline she wrote on the plane and typed out the opening sentence.

"How dare you?!" she screamed, turning red in the face as she faced her husband. His pants still strawn across the bedroom floor. Beside him, in her bed, was her best friend.

"It's not what it looks like!" she gasped.

Kate leaned back, admiring her opening sentences. It was juicy and straight into the conflict—and quickly gives all three characters a motive for murder.

Chapter 2

After two hours had passed, Kate looked around breathing a sigh. She needed something to drink. Something alcoholic, she decided. It was her holiday after all, and she thought she deserved it. Writing was hard. Getting the first paragraph down was even harder. She smiled, and noted that the bar queue was almost empty. Wasting no time, she made her way to the line, waiting for her turn to be served.

"What would you like?" the bartender asked her. He was tall, tanned and didn't appear any older than his mere twenties. A little young for her, but her characters would have a field day with him. All the looks of her character's preferences. She preferred a more mature gentleman who knew how to take care of her needs. She smiled, gazing around for a moment, before remembering the bartender had spoken to her. She still needed to choose a drink. "Ah... un rum and sprite, *por v'or*," she replied, doing her best spanish. He looked at her confused. She laughed nervously, and returned to her native tongue. "Rum and sprite, please."

He passed her the glass, topped with ice cubes and moved on to the next person behind her.

"Thanks," she muttered, feeling rushed aside.

She took a deep breath and went back to her seat. "Can I sit here?" a woman's voice asked.

Katie looked up. The woman was in her early to mid thirties, slender, with long red curly hair. She was holding a glass of what looked like coke, though she had no clue if anything was mixed in with it.

"Sure," Katie said, gesturing to the empty seat.

"What are you working on?"

That was a good question. "A murder mystery novel," she replied. "I'm just setting the scene before the body drops, though I am still deciding which one will be the one that drops dead. Could be the mistress, wife or husband. I'm leaning towards the mistress... but we'll see."

"Oooh, I do like a good mystery. What is it called?"

Katie laughed. "Book." she paused, smirking. "It doesn't have a title yet. I'll give it a title when the story is done."

A scream could be heard over at the pool, causing the women to look up briefly, followed by a large wave of water splashing out of the pool.

"If someone pushed me in the water, they are not my friend," the woman commented. Then turned and held out a hand towards her. "My name is Jenny by the way."

Katie smiled, taking her hand in reply. "Katie. How long are you staying for?"

"Two weeks, but I will go home at the end of this week."

"I just got here. I'm staying for one week. Looks like I'll be spending two days alone at the end. Shame."

Jenny nodded. "It's great here. Though, I wish I had relaxed a little more."

"What are you talking about? Have you not had a good time?"

"Oh, well, yeah, it's been lovely. But, me and my husband's brother had a falling out and it has caused some tension at home. I'm sure everything will go back to normal though as soon as we're home again and his brother has gone."

Katie nodded. "I can understand that. I'm not married myself, but I don't want to put myself in the position of being confronted in my own home—let alone on holiday when I am meant to be relaxing and having a good time."

She shrugged. "It happened. I'm over it. So, what are you drinking?"

Katie held up her rum and grinned. "I am drinking my fave. Rum. What about you?"

She laughed. "Rum by itself?"

"No! God no! It's mixed with coke. What about you?"

"No alcohol for me. I've just got coke."

Boring, Katie decided. "What's the point of being on holiday if you can't drink?"

Again, she shrugged. "I'm not bothered."

She stood from her seat, and waved at Katie before walking off. She wondered if she had offended her. It wasn't intentional. Sighing, she let it go and returned to her story, and her current predicament. Which character will she kill off? Perhaps, she should build a little more on the tension, and decide in the next chapter... Well, that was the plan. Somehow though, her plans had a bad habit of changing, and this time was no exception. She was about to type up the next sentence when a glass shattered from behind her.

Clouds darkened the sky. She closed her laptop and made her way back to the hotel. She can continue writing from the balcony, or at least, next to the balcony window, overlooking the ocean. As she reached her room, shouts echoed through the hall. She frowned and knocked on the door. The neighbours door swung open, and Jenny tearfully opened the door with a weak smile.

"Oh, hello again. Wha-What are you doing here?"

Katie raised an eyebrow. "I'm staying next door. Are you alright?"

She shook her head but said nothing. Katie took the hint. "Look, I'm gonna make some coffee. Do you want some?"

Jenny laughed lightly. "Have you tried their coffee? It isn't nice."

It was Katie's turn to laugh. "The hotel coffee? No. No, I brought my own. It's real coffee, freshly ground this morning. Do you want some?"

She beamed and closed the door behind her. "Yes please."

Katie opened her hotel room door and took off her shoes at the entrance before slipping on her slippers she had brought from home. Then, made her way to the kitchen and switched on her coffee machine. She could hear the water boil, before slowly dripping the black liquor into the large jug below. The aroma filled the room, and steam slowly rose from the caffeinated jug. Katie grabbed two of the mugs from the cupboard, and poured the contents into them, being careful not to spill any.

Rain poured down, slamming into every surface it could reach. The wind howled, and the tree branches swayed side to side, fighting not to topple over against the storm.

"I hope this doesn't last long," she mused.

Katie shrugged. "I like storms. It helps give my scenes a more sinister feel to it."

"Sinister indeed," she replied, swirling her coffee.

A knock on the door interrupted their conversation. Katie frowned and made her way towards it, pulling it open slowly.

"Who the fuck are you?" the man at the door demanded angrily.

"Speak to me like that again," she warned, "and I'm going to be your worst nightmare. Now, how about you tell me which one you are. The in-law, or the husband."

"She told you?"

"How could she not?" Katie retorted. "I was getting ready to call the cops. I don't like my friends being mistreated. So, again, who the fuck are you?"

He paused, eyeing her up to judge whether or not she was a threat to him.

"I'm her husband," he replied.

"Prove it."

"Wh-what?" he frowned.

"Prove it. I've not met you. And I'm not letting her go with some arsehole who demands it."

He cleared his throat, and pulled out his wallet. Inside, he pulled out a small photograph from behind his drivers licence. "See," he said, holding it out to her. "That's us."

She paused, studying it. It seemed legit.

"All right. Then you may come in and see her."

He nodded and pushed past her, down to the living room where Jenny was waiting.

"Babe, look, I'm sorry," he said, the moment he stepped through the door. "I don't know what got into me."

"Jealousy," she replied, folding her arms defensively. "I told you. Stop trying to split us up. It is not working."

"I'm not..." he insisted. "I'm trying to protect you!" Then handed her a large envelope. "He wants this signed," he said, softening his tone.

She opened the envelope and peered inside before closing it again. "Not whilst I'm on holiday. I'll take a look at it later."

He nodded. "I am so sorry for not listening to you. Look, I am gonna take him home. You enjoy the rest of the holiday, and I will meet you at the airport when you get back."

She sniffed back a tear and nodded, before they went their separate ways.

"I'm gonna need a stronger drink," she muttered.

Katie didn't hesitate, and immediately pulled out a bottle of wine and a bottle of rum from the fridge. "I have my stash right here. Take your pick."

Chapter 3

The next day came with somewhat of a contrast. The sun shone brightly, and dried up any evidence of the storm from the night before. She knocked on the door, and waited, holding a mug of freshly ground coffee. She paused, and waited. No sound. She knocked again, straining her ears for movement. Again no sound. Reluctantly leaving, she headed back to her room and got changed. She'll check on her new friend after getting some writing done.

She grabbed her laptop and the rest of her writing things, then headed out to the same spot as the day before, overlooking the ocean. The roaring waves that crashed against the shore, foaming over the sand, now gently waved with the tide.

She ordered herself a glass of ice water, and placed it on the table beside her laptop, though keeping it a good space to avoid spillages.

Katie began typing out the next words to her scene:

'The husband looked at his wife, pleading silently, though she could not face him. She turned away, bile rising in her throat. The thought of them, together, and in her bed... she shook the image from her head before turning towards them. "You both betrayed me. How long has this been going on?"

"Not long! A couple of weeks."

Weeks. She doubted that much. "Weeks or months?" she demanded again, turning towards her unfaithful husband. "Tell me the truth."

"Months," he whispered.

Her head spun. She felt another wave of nausea wash over her. "Get out," she said in a near whisper. "Get out. I never want to see either of you again."

She smiled to herself. The reader would be wondering, no doubt, whether she was sick, poisoned, or whether the shock of the betrayal had wounded her so badly, that it literally dropped her to her knees. Could she be dying from a broken heart? If this wasn't a murder mystery, she could almost pass it off as a bad romance.

Almost. She closed the lid to her laptop, and drank a glass of water. It was cold, and remnants of the ice cubes had floated to the surface. Condensation ran down the edges of the glass, dripping to the bottom, and formed a circular puddle on the table.

She returned to the hotel to get some food. The open buffet would be open soon for lunch. She smiled, and changed into lighter clothing to accommodate for the temperature rise. Her clothes stuck to her like... well, like glue. She peeled off her shirt and trousers, swapping it for a thin cotton buttoned down dress.

Then, headed to Jenny's door, knocking again. She banged on the door three times, as hard as she could. There was still no answer.

Sighing, there was no other option. After the argument from the previous day, she was worried. She hurried to the reception desk and waved down a woman holding a phone to her ear.

"Excuse me," Katie whispered. "I need some help."

The woman tucked her hair behind her ear, and ignored her. She frowned. Now was not the time for ignorance. She tapped loudly on the wood, impatiently. After what seemed like several minutes, the woman reluctantly met her disapproved gaze.

"Yes?"

"Finally!" Katie called out exasperated. "I've been trying to tell you, something is wrong! Jenny, from room twenty eight. I think something is wrong. She won't answer the door, and there was a massive falling out yesterday. I'm worried she did something stupid—or someone else did. Please, please... Can you check on her?"

She sighed, glancing down at the time. "Maybe she is a deep sleeper. Maybe she was up late. But, I'll send someone to check on her. You go and get some food."

Katie reluctantly agreed, though there was a feeling in the pit of her stomach that wouldn't shift.

She returned to her room, still unnerved by the absence of her friend. Perhaps a walk would calm her down. The receptionist might have been right. With the falling out yesterday, it wasn't out of the ordinary for someone to stay up late or go out to clear their head. She shook her head feeling foolish. Though, as foolish as she felt, the dread in her stomach only gripped on to her tighter.

Just as she was returning from her walk, she could see flashing lights reflecting from the road nearby. Sirens blared, growing louder the closer she got. Her blood froze, watching as a body bag was carried out of the door.

"No - no - no - no!" Katie gasped, rushing over towards them. "Please tell me it's someone from the ground floor. Any number except twenty eight. Please?"

The officer shook his head sadly. "I'm sorry. Did you know her?"

Katie nodded, unable to keep her voice from shaking. "She was my friend. What happened?"

He shrugged his shoulders, though his expression remained grim. "Looks like poisoning. Perhaps an overdose. We won't know until the autopsy. I would suggest, though, keeping your doors locked until we know more... and don't leave your drink unattended."

Common sense would agree. She blinked away her tears.

"She wasn't depressed," Katie told the officer tearfully. "It was just a falling out. She wouldn't have ended it. Please, sir. I think she was murdered."

He sighed, pointing towards her room. "Look, we'll look into it. Until then, please go inside and let us do our jobs."

Jobs. Like it was another Thursday. She pressed her lips together and closed the door behind her as she entered her room. They may not know her, but she did. And if she was a betting gal, she'd bet that her friend was murdered in cold blood—and her in-law had something to do with it.

KATIE SAT ON HER BED, deep in thought. How was she going to find out whether the in-law had killed her or not. Then again, it wouldn't make sense. Her brain hurt just thinking about it, recalling the conversation from the night before. She said the in-law "wanted his life" and wanted her to choose him. So, why kill her? Unless, of course, he came to the decision that if he couldn't have her, then no one can. Is that what happened? She felt sick. She needed to find out.

She opened her hotel room door, and listened for anyone that might want to stop her. She inched herself closer to Jenny's room, and pulled out her key to force open the door. It wasn't hard. With a slight angled card, she heard a click and then pulled the door open, ducking beneath the yellow tape reaching across the door frame.

Inside, she could smell what appeared to be bleach. She frowned, wondering if blood was found. Inspecting the surface, she lowered herself to all fours, looking for any signs of something more than poison or an opioid overdose. She was upset, but she certainly wasn't suicidal. She manoeuvred herself over to the cupboards, carefully opening the doors. It would help if she knew what poison was used. She frowned. There was nothing in the plate cupboards, and there was nothing in the sink. She continued on with the cleaning board and froze. Rat poison was sitting right at the front. Her stomach turned. There was no evidence of rodents in the room, but perhaps that was what the bleach was for. She needed to dig deeper. In the corner of the room, the small waste bin was half filled, sitting beside the bed in the next room. She stood, and began to make her way over to it.

"Stop right there!" a male voice commanded in a gruff voice. She recognised the voice immediately, and turned to face the detective. "What are you doing here? This is a crime scene!"

She cleared her throat.

"Is it? Because you wouldn't tell me. How did my friend die? Do you know what poison was used yet?"

He sighed, scratching his stubbly cheek. "Yes. Now, get out of here or I'm going to arrest you for interfering with a murder investigation, and messing with the evidence!"

She groaned, and lowered her head. "So, it was murder. I was right. In that case, I think we need to have a conversation."

"About what? Do you know who did this?"

She shrugged her shoulders. "I have a suspect in mind. She had a falling out with her in-laws. When was she killed?"

"Look," he said impatiently. "If you have someone in mind, tell me. But I can not be telling you about the investigation whilst it is still under way."

She supposed this was true, not that she liked being left in the dark.

"The husband and the brother in law," she told him with a sigh. "There was a falling out. He passed her a large envelope, it should be on the small table beside the bathroom door... that's where I saw her put it down last... unless she moved it since then... It wasn't until almost eleven at night that he actually listened to her. After, we had some rum and then she went home. I haven't seen or heard from her since. I thought she was sleeping it off, but when there was still no movement, I asked the woman at the desk to check on her."

"So, you were one of the last to see her alive?"

Again, she shrugged. "That would depend on when she died. Do you have a time of death?"

"Thank you for letting me know, now I need you to get out. I will look into it."

She sighed. Grumbling as she left the room. She paused in the doorway, and tilted her head slightly. She pointed towards the stairs, and frowned. "What's that?"

He frowned and knelt down beside where Katie was standing. A small smudge of blood was smeared on the lower frame of the door. "It might not be anything." He said, dismissively. "Someone probably stubbed their toe."

She frowned. She hadn't considered that. "Maybe..." she mused.

"Look. If she was killed and banged up, then what would be the point of her being poisoned?"

"Maybe the poison wasn't working fast enough? Maybe she refused to take it? Maybe he tried to dispose of her body?" Kate flailed her arms, getting more and more worked up. She rolled her eyes. "I don't know!" Katie ran her fingers through her hair in frustration. None of the evidence was adding up.

Chapter 4

Kate made her way to the bar, trying to remember more of the conversation she had with Jenny. She had glimpses of memories of them talking about her book, and the premise of one of the characters being killed off. She paused, and blinked. Perhaps, this was a way to make her friend immortal. Immortal and truly alive in the pages of her tales. She smiled, thinking how her friend would react to that if she were still alive. Suddenly, she had a new main character.

She grabbed her bag from her hotel room and pulled out her laptop. She had writing to do. And under the guise of the novel, she may find a way to bring Jenny's killer to justice.

There was a storm brewing. She could feel it in her bones. The promise of rain, given by the dark clouds looming over the city. Jenny had slept poorly all week, feeling the familiar aches and pains that age had plagued her with. That, and the reminder of when she was shot on duty last fall. Thankfully, it wasn't too serious and only nicked a bone. Though, unfortunately, it had caused some discomfort when the weather becomes damp or cold. She hugged her cup of coffee with both of her hands, warming herself before heading to work. She worked in Homicide, and the last case had her rattled. Her phone rang, startling her to the point of spilling her drink. "Sake," she muttered. She placed her cup on the table and answered the phone.

"Jenny, a body had just been reported. You need to come to Starlight Hotel. We're in room twenty-four."

She sighed, and pinched the bridge of her nose. "All right. I am on my way." She poured her coffee into a thermal mug and hastily made her way to the car. Whatever happened in the hotel, she had a feeling that it was not going to be something she would forget.

Katie smiled, and looked around. It was well into the night, nearing the early hours of the morning. Tomorrow, she would be starting an investigation of her own—and Jenny would be the one to solve it.

She slipped her laptop beside her bed and laid down. Her last thoughts were of Jenny, and her killer. If she can help it, her face will be the last one they'll see before prison.

The next morning, she woke up and grabbed her notepad from her bag, along with her favourite blue pen. There was work to be done. She poured herself a coffee into her thermal mug and got changed into her dress before heading out of the room. The hall was empty, though there was something seemingly off with the atmosphere. It was quiet. Too quiet for that time of day, at least. She made her way down to the bar, knowing that Jenny had spent a lot of time down there, watching the entertainment. That, and the endless supply of Cola.

She walked up to the bar, ordering herself a lemonade, and then leaned forward, glimpsing at the name label on the bartender's shirt.

"Hello there," she said, sighing. She rested her elbow on the table and propped up her chin, her hand balled into a loose fist.

"Have you heard the news?" she asked, watching his reaction.

"What news?" he asked. The bartender had curly black hair, with piercing bright blue eyes.

"My friend was murdered. She loved coming here..." she stated, letting her words trail off.

"Murdered? Here?" the bartender gasped. "Who was your friend?"

She nodded, and pulled out her phone, revealing the picture of them drinking rum in the hotel room.

"Her name was Jenny. She was my best friend... What am I gonna tell her kids?" she gasped. Her eyes teared up, a little trick she learned back in high school.

"Hey, I've seen her a couple days ago! She was murdered?"

Katie nodded.

The bartender shook his head in dismay. "She was lovely. It's a shame her husband filed for a divorce during her first day here."

She blinked, and took a deep breath. Of course, best friends would be privy to this conversation.

"YES, IT REALLY PUT a damper on her holiday. I know her brother in law had been trying to split them up for a while... he was under the impression that he was entitled to be with her, since they shared everything else—being twins an' all."

"What are you talking about?" he frowned. He straightened his back. "They've not spoken in months."

Taken aback, she frowned and straightened her back, gaining some distance between herself and the bar.

"Months? No, they were all together before she died. He was demanding to know why she was flirting with him, and she hadn't. It caused a huge row."

He laughed. "Now, I know you're not really her best friend. You barely know her. So, you tell me. What do you really know?"

Katie groaned. Figured he knew something she didn't.

"All right. Fine, you got me. I barely know her. We were friends for a couple of days—but what I said is true. There was an argument, and she came into my room. We had drinks, and then her husband came to the room to yell some more. I asked him to prove who he was, because I'd never met him and I wasn't about to hand her over to someone who had no business talking to her. He pulled out their wedding picture from behind his driving licence."

"It was behind his driver's licence... Are you sure?" the bartender asked.

Katie nodded. "I was right there when he pulled it out, and then I got Jenny and they argued about the in-law making moves. He said he was gonna take him home and that they'd meet at the airport when they get back."

The bartender fell silent. "If it was behind his licence, then that wasn't her husband. That was the in-law."

Katie gasped. Had she inadvertently led her to her death. "No, that can't be right. The brother in law surely doesn't look all that similar to her husband, right?"

"Lady," he said with a frown, "the brothers are identical twins."

"Even so," Katie argued. "I am sure she can tell her husband apart from her in law."

He shrugged. "Sober, perhaps. But she had three double martinis and cokes the other night. I doubt she would be able to tell them apart when she can't see straight. I had to send someone to escort her to her room."

She sat down, massaging her brow. "She told me it was just cola. After that drink, we got through half a bottle of rum." She let the realisation sink in. Not only did she lie, but she was intoxicated to boot. There was no way she would have known who she was talking to, and didn't see him take the picture from his wallet. Which left another question hanging in the air.

"So, if that was the in-law, what happened to her husband?"

"My best guess," the bartender stated. "I'd reckon he would be at home."

She asked for another drink as she contemplated the situation. Why would she lie to her? It wasn't like she had a reason to suspect anything at that point. Not to mention the divorce, which seemed sketchy as well. Why divorce her on the first day of holiday... "unless," she thought in horror "the husband knew she was going to die..."

"What was that?" he asked, frowning.

Katie shook her head. "Listen, do you know if she signed the papers?"

He shrugged. "I have no idea. Why?"

"It seems sketchy to divorce her on holiday. But, if the husband expected her to sign the papers after the holiday—and have her killed before she signs it, he'd still claim on her life insurance. So, I need to find those papers—before he has a chance to."

Everything was getting messy, and fast. Which also meant she would have to return to her hotel room—and risk being arrested. She only hoped that it wouldn't be in vain.

She paid the bartender, and looked at the name tag again. She needed to remember it. It was important, and at the same time, not make it look like she was looking. He's just another face, she reminded herself.

"All right..." she sighed. "Time to pay another visit to Jenny's room. Be a dear and don't tell the cops. I want to find proof before I tell them."

He chuckled, shaking his head. "Look, I'm not going to go out of my way to tell them, but I won't lie either. Do what you must, but I would suggest maybe not going into her room. It's sealed, and it would be a crime."

She frowned. It is sealed. But, if he had been behind the bar, then how could he possibly have known that? The last she looked, it was only taped across the doorway. Which meant, she realised...horror grew in the pit of her stomach. She turned away from him, walking towards the door as she finished her thought. "He was there recently. But why?" Only one reason came to her, that would be a reasonable explanation. He was looking for someone, or something. Perhaps even the divorce papers... It also dawned on her that if the bartender was part of the mystery, she may have just put herself right in the crosshairs. And, possibly, a threat on her life. She swallowed hard. This mystery was becoming much more complex than the ones in her stories, and everyone is hiding a secret.

Chapter 5

Kate dragged her feet as she reluctantly made her way back to her room, with her thoughts on the case spinning around and around in her head, teasing her. There was something she wasn't seeing, a truth hidden within the lies. She pinched the bridge of her nose. What *was* the truth? Did she have Cola in her glass, or was it something more? How did he know about the divorce, if there was one. Nothing made sense anymore, and it was driving her crazy.

As she approached the door to her room, she noticed someone standing outside her door. She paused, and ducked into a doorway for a look. The half hidden figure, the other half hidden from her view, revealed that he was an officer: A constable, she reckoned. She frowned, scanning the intruder's stance. Sitting at his belt, was a holster. The cop was concealing a gun. Her frown deepened, and she strode over to her door, preparing for what's to come.

"I hope you have a warrant, or a written invitation to be in my room," she announced.

The constable scanned her with his beady eyes. "We have permission," he grunted.

"You better," she snipped back. "And it better be a warrant, because I sure as hell didn't send out an invite."

The detective emerged from the living room, holding up a small glass mug. "I believe we have everything we need," he declared, glaring at her. She stared back, hardening her resolve. "You wanted a mug?"

"Your mug," he corrected. "With your fingerprints all over it."

"Well obviously," she replied defensively, "it's my room!"

He smirked, as though she had just declared him a winner of some competition. "Exactly."

She shook her head. She was too tired for this shit. "What are you talking about?"

He pulled out another mug, matching the one in his hand. "I got this one from Jenny's room. Guess how many fingerprints were found on it."

She didn't need to guess, but she didn't like his attitude. "Unless you used gloves for that, I'm going with three."

"Two," he snarled. "Jenny's and yours. Care to explain?"

She shrugged. "Are you having trouble putting two and two together?"

"Tell me."

She took a deep breath. "We had coffee. Obviously."

He looked at her, dumbfounded. "Coffee," he repeated.

"Yes. She was having a rough day, and I offered her coffee. I used the mug from my room. She went back to her own room, with the so-called husband. It's not like I put rat poison into it."

They froze, and their jaws dropped. Stupid woman, she scolded herself. They hadn't known she went into that room, and now they have reason to think she did it. She closed her eyes, letting out a deep breath of frustration. She barely heard the next words that came out of his mouth.

"You're under arrest for the suspicion of murder."

"Of course," she muttered. "It's not like this holiday was going well anyway."

Katie was led into the police station, with the cuffs bounding her wrists together behind her back. The metal links dug into her skin, pinching her with each movement. She winced, but said nothing. They would pay soon enough, she was sure. And then, they would be asking for her help. Of course, she wasn't about to give them the information now, not after the way they have treated her.

"What's the charge," the receptionist asked, keeping her eyes on the screen in front of her.

"Suspicion of murder," he stated, puffing out his chest proudly.

"I'm innocent, but whatever," she remarked.

The detective ignored her and continued to tap at the keyboard.

They took her picture and then took her into a small room, with a mattress not thicker than a rug.

"You'll have me out of here with a huge apology, and a coffee, when you realise what an idiot you've been."

"I doubt it," he remarked.

It didn't take long for her to be proven right. She sat in the cell, twiddling her thumbs as she took in the details. As a writer, how could she not? What better time to view the cell from the other side of the door.

She smiled, wishing that she had a notepad or a sketch book. Will they allow her to take a few pictures before she is released? She hoped so.

The detective walked away from the cell door, bolting it shut. "Crazy assed woman," he muttered to no one in particular.

"What?" his partner frowned, catching the last gasp of his mutter.

"Oh, nothing," he replied quickly. "I was talking to myself."

She rolled her eyes. "Well then, how about you close this case properly before dismissing her as crazy. All we have is circumstantial evidence. This won't hold up long in court, especially with the judge."

He grunted his agreement. "Yeah, well. Now that she's in the cell, we can search her room a little more thoroughly," he stated.

"James, we did that already. We had the warrant for it, remember?"

She looked at him, arching her eyebrow, and watching his expression. "Right?"

"Of course we had a warrant. We wouldn't have been allowed in if we hadn't."

"And the affidavit included her drawers?"

He frowned. "I didn't look through her drawers, just her kitchen. It was all we needed."

She looked unconvinced, but shrugged it off. "All right then. So, where exactly are you looking to search through next?"

He shrugged. Honestly, he hadn't thought that far ahead. "I'm just gonna go broad and say the whole room - to be on the safe side. In case anything comes up unexpected."

"The judge won't like that,"

His phone rang during lunch. He put down his sandwich, almost wishing he hadn't taken a bit of the tuna before picking up the phone.

"Hello," he said, with half a mouthful.

"Uh, what?" came a reply. It was the receptionist.

James swallowed and tried again. "Hello," he repeated. "What's up?"

"The switchboard just called. There's been another body."

"But, we were just there," he frowned. "What do you mean there has been another body? Where?"

"You just been at the Robin Hood Resort cabin?"

"Cabin? No. The hotel. What happened at the cabin?"

She sighed. "I just told you. There's been another body. Go to room twenty."

He hung up the phone and cussed. He really should have eaten his sandwich, there'll be no time to eat it now. "What a waste," he muttered.

He turned to his partner, who was standing at the coffee machine. "Liz, make it a coffee-to-go, we gotta go."

"Go where?" she frowned.

"The cabin of that resort. There's another body."

She sighed, and poured her coffee into a polyester cup and sealed it with a plastic lid. "All right. Let's go."

It puzzled him that the body was so close to the original crime scene. He reasoned that she could have committed the murder right before they turned up. Or, and this thought troubled him greatly, the crazy assed woman could be telling the truth, and he would owe her a big assed apology along with a big-assed cup of coffee. "Please, let it be older than the original murder," he prayed.

"What?" Liz frowned.

"Nothing," he muttered again. "I just hope we got the right person for this, is all."

"Relax," she laughed. "It could be a coincidence. It might not be connected at all."

"In the same resort? I hardly think so."

Though, he thought bitterly, with the way his day was going, he doubted it.

Chapter 6

The cabin was closed off when he got there, with the security guards watching the entrances warily.

"Ok, gentlemen," he said, greeting them with a false smile. "What have you got for me?"

"Uh…" the first guard stammered. "D-Did you have something to eat?"

"I had a bite. Why?"

"Ok. Well, you can count your lucky stars then. Brace yourself."

He straightened his back, preparing for whatever was inside.

The first thing he noticed was the stench of blood. The carpet was crumpled up, and there were footprints belonging to some large shoes heading up the hall, leading into the room ahead.

"What's over there?" he asked.

The security cleared his throat. "The victim," he replied.

"I said, what. Not who?"

"Oh. It's the bathroom, sir."

He frowned.

He made his way over to the bathroom, dreading what he may find.

He could hear his footsteps echoing against the wooden floorboards, the kind of echo you would hear in a new, or old house. It was hollow, and felt as though he was trespassing somewhere forbidden. The hair on the back of his neck stood on end. The smell of blood grew stronger, the closer he got.

With a nudge of his elbow, being careful not to touch anything, he pushed the door open.

Inside, a man was sitting on the toilet. His trousers were still sitting at his ankles, with his hands placed between his legs. Detective James cleared his throat, remembering the scene from the Game of Thrones television series. His eyes moved up, towards his torso. His shirt was ruffled, with only one arm in its sleeve. He had either tried to put his shirt on, or take it off. That was a given - or at least, someone had. The red cotton was torn at the collar. This whole scene didn't make sense. "What the hell happened here?" James frowned, his eyes wide. His eyes moved up again. The cause of death, he figured. His throat was severed, almost taking his head clean off his shoulders. The man's face, distorted into a silent scream. Blood drained from his face, and the white bloodless corpse was all that was left.

"Ok, so this is a strange one. But, why did you think that this was related to my hotel case?" he asked.

The security guard shuffled his feet nervously. "You mentioned poison, right?"

"Uh, yeah. Rat poison," he replied, failing to see any links to poisoning at all. "Where? I mean, the cause of death was clearly from the cut throat."

The security moved the victim's hands from his crutch, revealing a small vial in place of where his manhood was meant to be. The label of the contents had been removed, though, one remained - no doubt, on purpose. He used his gloves, removing the object from the body, getting a closer look at what the label read. "Toxic," he read in a flat tone. "Oh." It took him a minute to process what he was seeing, before his train of thought ended. "Wait. If the vial of poison was in place of his dick... then where the hell is the rest of him?"

"In here, sir."

He pointed to the victim's mouth.

He frowned, even more confused. "What?"

The security guard took a step back. "There's a reason his mouth is open that wide, sir."

The sheer thought that followed left him cold to the bone. "You have got to be kidding me." He stepped to where the security guard had been standing, and leaned in for a closer look. "Oooh," he groaned again. Then cleared his throat. "Well, we have good news and we have bad news," he stated, taking a step back himself.

"What's that?" the guard frowned, looking a little green.

"Well, this is definitely unrelated to my case. That's the good news. The bad news is that someone is gonna have to stand here a while longer, for another detective to come out."

He wished the security good luck and got on the phone to the station, updating them on the case. Then, hanging up, he returned to his car, and shuddered, unable to get the image of his dick shoved down the full length of his throat - including the two meat.

"I need a drink," James muttered. "I should never have taken this case."

His colleague laughed.

The drive back was a long one. The scene haunted him, refusing to release the detective from its grip.

"So, what's your thought moving forward?" Liz asked.

James sighed. "Well, since that was unrelated - as bad as it was, the prime suspect is still on Katie. But to know for sure, I am going to have to find out the time of death - and I mean, really narrow it down, and see whether or not she was with the victim, or whether she was telling the truth; which would then mean finding witnesses to collaborate to that effect."

"So, you still think she did it."

"Yes. I still think she did it - and what's more, I think she planned it from the beginning."

"P-planned the murder? She only just arrived," Liz argued.

"I think the only thing that was a variable in this, would be Jenny. It could have been anyone else. Why else would you take your own coffee? It'd be harder to trace. And, being a writer and all, perhaps she got bored with creating fake scenes, and decided to make one of her own...for her story or something."

"That... seems like a stretch," Liz commented.

Honestly, so did he. But at this point, it was all he had.

KATIE WAS BEGINNING to get restless in her cell. The room felt cold, and restricted. She supposed it was meant to feel that way; given the bright white walls, and the steel door that separated her cell to the world outside.

The guards were heard muttering and mumbling a conversation with each other, though their words failed to reach her ears. She pushed herself to the tips of her toes. Words were meaningless; body language, however, spoke many columns.

The first guard, the one with the keys to her imprisonment, was leaning back against the back of his chair, casually swinging from side to side. His hands, waving a dismissive gesture at whatever he was being told. He wasn't taking the news seriously, if at all. His partner though, shuffled his feet along the floor. His hands and arms were animated as he paced the full length of the desk. He was upset, and struggling to calm himself down: a sign of something getting into his bonnet. His colleague didn't seem to be reassuring him. Whatever it was, Katie was sure she was about to hear all about it - either in her cell, with yet another accusation, or from the news - on the off chance that they'd turn on the radio.

"Hey, guard? What got your friend's knickers in a twist?" Katie asked. What else was she to do? She was bored!

"He lost your Mum's number," he snapped, his tone thick with sarcasm.

"Ooh" she said, mocking him. "Does he want to be my new daddy?"

The guard coughed and spluttered, spitting out his coffee, spraying it everywhere. "Wh-what?!"

"Don't worry about it," she smirked. "She has probably already forgotten his name, anyway."

Chapter 7

Detective James walked in, practically tugging at his hair. The coroner was standing over the victim of what used to be Jenny.

"Do we have a time of death yet?" he asked, trying not to get too close.

"Hello, James," she greeted with a false smile.

"Oh. Hi. Sorry," he said, a little apologetic.

"Please. Do you have a time of death?"

"Yeah, actually," she told him. She passed him a sheet of paper. "Well, contrary to what we thought, she died a lot later than we suspected."

"What? How much later?"

She cleared her throat. "She died at six in the morning."

"Noo," he groaned. "That means that my only suspect is innocent!"

"You better let her out then," she told him. "Especially if she didn't do it."

He grunted. He already knew that she had left the premises at six, and she was seen leaving and arriving at the bar. "Yeah," he muttered. "I better get her a coffee, along with a large helping of an apology."

"Before you do that," she continued, pushing a strand of her hair out of her face, she passed him another sheet of paper.

"What's this?" he asked, waving it about.

"The actual poison for her death."

"Rat poison," he stated.

She frowned. "How did you know?"

He sighed. "Because it was in her kitchen cupboard." He paused, and frowned. "And, I just realised that my prime suspect may not have killed her, but she still broke the law."

"What do you mean?" she asked.

He was already walking away as he spoke. "She went into an active crime scene!"

He walked into the station, and took a glimpse of the guards standing by the desk.

"What the hell is going on here?" he demanded, staring at the spilled drink all over the desk. Kate was looking a little too pleased with herself.

"What did you do?" he demanded, glaring at her.

She shrugged. "They were telling me how they want to have relations with my mother. They didn't like my reply."

"What reply?"

"Nothing much," she retorted with a smirk. Her eyes moved past him towards Jenson. "Isn't that right... Daddy."

Jenson coughed and spluttered, looking embarrassed and lost of words. "I-I..."

"That's enough," the detective exclaimed. "You're all behaving like children!"

She arched an eyebrow. "Have you come to let me go?" she asked, leaning against the wall of her cell.

"No," he replied, a little too quickly. "I'm not. You may not have killed the woman, but you're still getting charged."

It was her turn to splutter, and turn red. "For what?" she demanded.

"Trespassing, and contaminating an active crime scene."

She snorted. "Barely criminal. You weren't doing your job, so I did. When you let me go, with an apology and a large coffee, I might let you know what I found when I was there."

"You'll tell me now."

She laughed, shaking her head. "How about, I meet you halfway?"

He paused. What would she consider as half way?

"What?"

"You buy me a large coffee, and bring me my laptop, and I'll tell you what you want to know."

"Coffee, and... your computer?" he repeated. "That's all? No more bidding for freedom?"

"Look," she replied indignantly. "I refuse to be charged for a crime I didn't commit. The reason I'm in here. But, for something I genuinely did, I'll take my lumps. All I want is my coffee and my laptop."

"Your coffee, not one from the store?"

"*My* coffee," she repeated. "The ones *you* all drink taste like shit."

SHE WATCHED AS HE LEFT the room. "All right," he muttered, before closing the door. "But I want everything."

"And you will have it," she replied.

Kate sighed, already imaging the welcoming aroma of real coffee - rather than the instant stuff the hotel offered.

It took less than ten minutes to return with her stuff. He placed it on a table in front of her, and waited. She placed the ground coffee in the filter, making sure there was enough for more than one mug. Then switched on her laptop - still over half a battery. She smiled. "Thank you," she began, "Put this in the machine, and push the green button. In the meantime, whilst it's doing its thing, we'll have a conversation about everything I saw in that room."

He followed her instructions, placing the coffee machine at the far end of the room. Then took a seat in front of her.

"All right. Let's get started. What did you see, and this better be good?"

"Have you spoken to the bartender?" she began.

He frowned. "What has he got to do with it?" he demanded, irritably. "Was he in the room?"

She smiled. "Trust me, you'll want to answer the question. It'll make sense."

"Ugh. He said he didn't know her."

"Interesting. Because, before I went into that room, I spoke to the bartender. I told him about her being my best friend, and how the bar was her favourite spot, and how devastated I was about her death. He couldn't recall her name, so I showed a picture. Then, he remembered. Now, pending on the blood work - it'll determine who the killer is."

"Now, I am confused."

"Trust me, so am I," she confessed. "Especially when he told me that Jenny and her husband hadn't spoken for a while, and that he'd asked her for a divorce the first day of the holiday."

"What does that have to do with anything?" he demanded. "Lots of people get divorces."

"Yeah, but, I hadn't met the husband. And he has a twin brother. He also told me that Jenny was intoxicated on the day that she was murdered. She told me she only had cola in her glass."

"I'm still not understanding."

She frowned. "Two things. If she hadn't spoken to her husband for a while, why wait for the first day of holiday to ask her for a divorce? Secondly, if she was intoxicated, how could she tell the difference between them - especially after not seeing each other for a while. Thirdly, and the point."

"Finally," he muttered.

"How does the bartender know she was asked for a divorce, he didn't even know her name? And if the husband had in fact asked for a divorce, then where are the papers?" She continued on, her words rambling out with no sign of stopping. "So, either the brother in law impersonated her husband, or he had her killed. You ask for a divorce on the first day of holiday, not to give her time to process or ruin her trip. But if he had taken the papers, there'd be no sign of divorce at home - so, if she was killed on holiday, who's to say they ever had issues - and then claim on her life insurance. It might even be the case that he killed her because she didn't want him. And maybe, it was the brother in law that could have asked for the divorce, so he could claim her as his. See what I'm getting at?"

He looked at her like she had lost her mind. "Uh, ye - no. I have no clue what you're talking about."

"It's simple. Check her blood work. If she was loaded, then she wouldn't be thinking or seeing straight. And unless he asked for divorce in public, then how does the bartender know about it. He could have gone in her room. There is a lot of suspects in this, but we can narrow it down by finding out whether or not she drank!"

"And if she didn't drink?"

"Then, why would the bartender lie?"

He removed his glasses with a groan. "I really *really* shouldn't have taken this case," he muttered.

Chapter 8

Kate couldn't shake the feeling that she was forgetting something. It was a long day, and she had an even longer day waiting for her. Until the real killer was caught, there was no way she would be allowed to go home. She sighed and pinched the bridge of her nose.

"What am I missing?" she frowned. She thought back to all of the times she had spent with Jenny, and wondered what she would do if she was in the same situation. If it had been her instead.

"Have you spoken to the other neighbours?" she asked, tapping her finger on her chin.

"Of course," James replied. "I have been doing this for some time, you know."

She shook her head, ignoring the bitter tone in his voice. "What did they say?"

"Nothing," he told her. "They were either asleep, or out. Though, they did mention that the jousting event was interesting."

"Jousting?" she frowned. She had gone jousting with her just days before her murder. Did she recall anything odd? She rattled her brains, trying to remember what had happened. The decoration was on point, and the edge of the arena was lined with small shields. On the left, there was a guy holding and handing out the javelin, swords and armour. "I guess the guy handling the equipment was a little nervous, but he could have been new."

"Nervous how?" he replied.

She shrugged. "He fumbled a bit when he was picking out the weapons. At one point, an arrow flew in our direction - but it wasn't like it was on purpose..."

"That you know of," he stated. Kate watched as he wrote the mention into his notepad. "Would you trust an inexperienced person to be handling weapons in a crowd of people?"

He had her there. "I guess not," she replied with a heavy sigh. "I guess we better go and take a look."

She hated the thought that he might be right, but she would hate herself more if she hadn't looked into it at all. She shook her head. In this case, she hoped that he was wrong - but the questions had to be asked. Why was he so nervous at the performance?

"Are we going to go and see him now?" she asked, frowning. It had been a long day already, and nearing eleven. He sighed and turned his attention briefly to his watch fastened to his left wrist.

"I suppose not. We'll go first thing in the morning. That'll give you time to get some sleep, and wash up before we go."

She offered him a small smile and thanked him. Then, turned towards the direction they came from, and hesitated. "Which way is back to the hotel?" she asked with a frown.

He sighed again, reluctantly gesturing towards the car. "Come on," he said. "I'll take you back."

She thanked him again, and climbed back into the car on the passenger side.

They made it back to the hotel just before midnight. He walked her over towards the receptionist and leaned in, showing his badge. "Excuse me. I don't suppose this lady still has a room available?"

The red-haired receptionist pushed up her glasses and tapped a few keys on the keyboard. "I-I'm sorry. After you escorted her out, we assumed she didn't need it anymore. We've already given her room to someone else."

Katie looked back at James with disbelief. "What do you mean you gave away my room?!" Katie snapped, turning her attention to the receptionist. "What did you do with my stuff?!"

The red-head cleared her throat, checking the system once again. "It's... uh... In the lost and found room. I'll go and get it."

She scurried away, with Katie opening her mouth to comment more.

"Great," she muttered. "See what you've done?" she said, accusingly. "Now where am I gonna sleep?"

"What do you mean there are no spaces?" Detective James demanded. He ran his hand through his hair, trying not to rip it out.

"I - I can have a look in the system for the next available slot..." she stuttered, tapping feverishly at the keyboard. She paused and straightened out her glasses, as she tried to gain some sort of control over the situation. "There is a space available in a week. Would you like the same room you were in?" she asked.

Kate rolled her eyes and leaned her head against the desk. "Yes. Fine. whatever."

"I expect her full holiday to be reimbursed," the detective stated coolly. "Since this was meant to be a holiday, and instead had been detained briefly, and cut-short by your error."

She nodded nervously. "Yes, of course. I'll speak to my manager about it."

"You do that," he snipped. "If she disagrees, I am sure you can give her my number."

"Yes, yes..." she agreed hurriedly. She booked the room, and watched as the Detective turned back to Kate scowling at him. "Well, that's next week dealt with. But where am I going to sleep tonight?" she demanded. "Everything else would have been booked months ago." Kate's eyes watered, turning away to hide the tears threatening to escape.

"Look," he said with a defeated sigh. "I got you into this mess... You can come and stay with me."

She blinked, her tears stopped abruptly - overridden by confusion. "What?" she gasped. As if the absurd-ury wasn't clear enough. Did she hear him right? She cleared her throat. "You lost me my place in the hotel, completely destroyed my holiday by your incompetence, and now you want me to stay at your house?"

"I am trying to help fix this," he replied sharply. "So, stop complaining and get into the car."

She let out a long frustrated sigh. If Jenny was still alive, she was sure that she'd have something to say about it; but what?

The journey back was filled with tension. The back of the car seat felt rigid, sticking into the base of her spine. Her head, almost touching the roof, bounced from the ceiling with each speedbump they came across. She was sure he had done it on purpose.

After what felt like a ride across jagged rocks, they finally slowed to a stop outside a small little house. It wasn't what she expected. For some reason, she assumed the house that the detective would be living in would be a dingy flat in a tower block. Instead, she was standing in front of a charming little cottage, complete with a white picket fence.

"You have got to be kidding," she scoffed, climbing out of the car. "Surely you don't live here?"

"What?" he frowned, daring her to comment more. "Problem?"

"No. No," she replied flippantly. "But, this looks like it would belong to your grandmother," she laughed.

He looked at her, dead serious, in the eye. "It did," he stated, with a tense edge to his tone. "And she left it to me. Now, come on inside." He walked down the cobbled pathway and unlocked the door. The door was barely half open before he turned towards her again, hesitating before he spoke. "Oh," he said, as though he had remembered something of importance, "be sure to take your shoes off at the door. I don't want you to be bringing mud into my nice clean house. This is my home, not a farmhouse - and I want you to respect my space."

She watched him for a moment, and nodded. He opened the door the rest of the way with a gentle push, revealing a lush red carpet in the hallway, with pictures scattered across both walls. Each photo captured a precious memory of him and his nan, going right back to when he was a young boy.

She leaned in closed towards a small picture. The young detective was wearing a flat hat and holding a bubble-blowing pipe in one hand, its tip hanging from between his lips, and a magnifying glass grasped tightly in his hand. She chuckled. "Let me guess, your first case?"

His eyes darted towards the image, and back at her. "No," he replied shortly. "It was my third."

"Third? What was the case?"

He sighed, and he turned his attention to the photograph. His eyes glazed over, getting lost in a memory from long ago. "Her ring had fallen off her finger from when she lost weight... so, I went to find it." He fell silent for a moment before continuing. "It was important, because it was her wedding band - and the last reminder of her husband - my grandfather - so, I took it very seriously."

Kate bit her lip. "I'm sorry. I was just teasing..."

"I know," he replied, shaking his head. "But you shouldn't make snap judgments. You of all people should know that," he snapped. "Like my snap judgement of you, for a killer."

She cleared her throat again, feeling somewhat foolish. "I'm sorry."

Chapter 9

Detective James led her into the living room and gestured towards the sofa. It was pure black leather, and a soft almost-new rug in the centre of the room that circled the small coffee table as a centrepiece.

"This is an odd little setup," she commented, smiling.

He shrugged. "Yeah, but it's not like I normally have company over to make comments on it."

"Touche," she replied. "Still, I like it."

He offered her a little smile, then pointed towards the kitchen door at the end of the room. "Coffee?" he asked.

She nodded, pleased that he had offered her something hot to drink, rather than water. "Thanks, that'd be great," she replied. She slipped off her coat and clutched her overnight bag to her chest. "Where would I be sleeping?" she asked, cautiously.

HE LOOKED AT HER FOR a moment, then laughed. "Oh, right. Sorry... you can have the sofa."

Kate turned to take a closer look at the sofa she was sitting on. It was a three-seater. "Well, I suppose it's big enough for me to lie on..." she then turned sideways, judging the width. "It'll be a tight fit though..."

He sighed, putting his hands on his waist with a huff. "Do you want the bedroom then?" he demanded.

"Uh, no no. It's ok. I'm just saying it's a little narrow. I didn't mean to sound like I was complaining. I just don't want to fall off and make a lot of noise... it's no bother."

She sighed. How on earth did she get into this situation? She shook her head muttering to herself. "At this rate, I won't be coming back on holiday here... What a nightmare this has turned out to be."

"Pardon?" he snapped, his tone taking a hard edge to it.

"Nothing!" she cried out, laying down. "Just saying. This was meant to be a relaxing holiday, and bring inspiration for my next book... Instead, it has been stressful and somewhat disappointing. If I hadn't come—"

The detective carried the fresh coffee into the living room and placed it on the table in front of her. His tone softened a little when he spoke. "If you had not come, Jenny would still be dead. The killer would still be out there, and someone else would be sleeping on my couch, drinking my coffee."

"I suppose," she sighed. Not that it made her feel any better.

She grabbed the coffee mug off the table and took a sip. "If it makes you feel any better, you know how to make a nice cup of coffee."

He laughed. "Thanks," he said with a smile. "You can thank my nan for that too. She gave me the coffee machine to make it with."

She suppressed an inward groan. She was never going to live this down.

Katie woke in the middle of the night by the sound of foxes screaming in the garden out the front. She groaned, burying her head in her pillow. "Fuck sake," she muttered.

It seemed like hours before she fell back to sleep.

"Come on!" a male's voice snapped at her, nudging Kate in her shoulder.

She groaned, pulling her blanket over her head.

"I only just fallen asleep," she grumbled. "Gimme five more minutes..."

A reluctant huff sounded from behind her, with soft footsteps retreating towards the back end of the room.

"You have until the coffee is ready," he stated.

Coffee. Finally, something that made sense. She peeled back her eyelids, forcing the daylight into her sight.

"Ah!" she screamed, covering her eyes again. Blinding light burned her tired eyes from what she could only surmise to be the brightest bulb he could find.

Minutes passed a lot faster than she expected, with Detective James passing her a large mug of black coffee. The welcoming aroma wafted up her nose like a familiar friend.

"This ought to wake you," he muttered, taking a seat opposite her.

She nodded. "The foxes were fighting last night. Screaming off and on forever."

He nodded solemnly. "They do that a lot. Nothing much can be done though. Animals fight for food all the time. It's just the way it is."

She took a large gulp, feeling the liquid burn the back of her throat.

"That's good coffee," she said, re-establishing her comment from the night before. "But I wish I could sleep."

"Well, there's a killer on the loose, so you can sleep after they're caught."

She groaned, taking another large gulp. "Yeah, yeah," she huffed. She shook her head. Living in the lives of her characters wasn't nearly as fun or as interesting as she thought it would be. In her stories, they'd have a lead by now. Instead, they had just woken up. She frowned again, thinking. "If this were one of my books... I'd say we were in the early chapters. So, my characters would be looking at security footage, and talking to the staff members - with so many people milling around... something would have been noticed, right?"

He looked at her, raising his eyebrows. "If this was one of your stories?"

"Oh. Yeah, I'm a writer. It's why I came on holiday," she told him, perking up a little. Talking about her writing process always gave her a little boost of morale, even if the other person wasn't nearly as invested in the experience.

"This isn't a romantic," he frowned, eyeing her warily. "This is murder. This isn't a bonding moment, or segway into a romantic relationship. You know that, right?"

"I know," she replied. "And, I don't write romance. I write murder mysteries. And I came on holiday for relaxation and inspiration for my next book. And instead..."

"Instead, got involved in one?"

She nodded. "Yeah."

He chuckled lightly. "Well, what better source of inspiration? You have a case right here? Don't use the case details, but I'm sure the methods and questions would give you plenty to think about."

She thought for a moment. "You're right." She blinked, thinking. "Ok... I can do this. From your last case - without giving me any specifics, obviously, what was the murder weapon?"

He frowned. "That's what you want to start with?" he sighed. "It was a gun."

A gun. The thought echoed inside her head. It wasn't exciting. People get shot all the time. How can she use this for inspiration? She tilted her head to one side. "Follow up question: was it with or without a silencer?"

He barely looked at her as he took a large mouthful of his own coffee, then pulled a face. "Eugh. I forgot to put in the sugar."

"Detective? Silencer? Yay or nay?"

"Oh. Yeah, there was no attachment on the gun. The killer used a duvet to muffle the noise. It worked, because no one heard the shot."

A blanket? She looked away in disgust. Boring! Now, if the victim was naked - or even the killer was naked, she might be onto something. What an earth could her characters use for a silencer though? She couldn't very well copy them.

What else would muffle the sound of a gunshot?

The tiny taps of the water dripping, and landing into the empty sink irked her. Drip, drip, drip... it was enough to drive anyone insane.

"How are you not driven crazy by that tap? It's relentless."

He shrugged. "I've made calls about it, but I'm still waiting for repairs."

Drip drip drip. She ground her teeth together, trying to ignore it. Drip drip drip. A light bulb went off in her head. Inspiration or insanity? She wasn't sure. "Drip drip drip," she muttered, mostly to herself. "The blood can drip onto a hard surface, but be in a room that echoed..."

"What's that got to do with the murder weapon?" he frowned. She smirked. "The taps already gave us that answer."

"What? The sink?"

She laughed. "Nooo. Water," she beamed. "You know what resorts have plenty of?"

"Taps?"

She shook her head. "Pools! That's how the killer is gonna shoot. It's gonna be in the water. "

"Nope. Won't work," he said smugly. "The gun won't fire in the water. It can't get wet."

She pulled a face. "Really? Dang it! I thought I had something..."

He checked the time and signalled to the clock. "Take a shower, think about it, and then it's time to go."

Time to go my ass, she thought bitterly to herself. She switched on the timer, trusting whatever temperature the shower was set to, and hoped that she would make it out alive . Would it be a cold shower to start the day, or a hot one? She smirked to herself, picturing the detective stepping into the hot shower, with steaming rolling off his muscles as he exited the cubicle. She cleared her throat. Having those sort of thoughts would undoubtedly be a hindrance to the story line, rather than help. But then again... she thought coolly. What's wrong with a little bit of romance?

She emerged from the shower with water running down her back. Her hair falling down to her shoulder blades, feeling heavy on her head. She had considered getting it thinned out, if she had the time. But she would have to wait until she returned home.

She sighed. Home. It seemed so far away. She Grabbed a towel from the rack and wrapped it around her waist making sure that she was covered. "You done?" he asked, calling out to her. She smiled to herself before answering. "I am now," she told him. "I'm just grabbing some clean clothes from my bag and then I'll let you have your bathroom back."

He grunted his acknowledgment, and she glanced warily at the time. It wasn't even eight in the morning yet, at which point, she would normally be waking up from her sleep, feeling refreshed and ready to start the new day - after a shower of course. The Spanish heat already bared down on them, so threw on the first dress that she could get her hands on. A blue floral dress, that was light-weight, and her favourite style. Maxi. The maxi-dress reached down to her feet, and provided enough elastic to give her figure a bit of a curve in her otherwise flat torso.

"Ready?" he asked again.

She nodded, now dressed, as she walked into the lounge. The detective was also fully dressed, sipping at another cup of coffee. A much smaller cup. She frowned, watching him with a questioning look.

"What are you drinking from?" she asked, knowing the answer, but hoped he would take the hint.

"An espresso cup," he replied. He gulped it back and pulled a face.

"Don't suppose you made a second...?"

He chuckled and passed her a miniature sized cup. She eyed it, frowning. The cup was the size of her pinkie finger. She held the handle delicately between her thumb and forefinger, before smelling the coffee. The strong aroma greeted her with a face full of caffeine. "Smells like pure coffee," she smiled.

"It is. So, if you're ready to get to work, let's go."

She grumbled to herself, but gulped back the espresso, feeling the instant caffeine hit.

"Woza!" she gasped.

He laughed and opened the door, watching as she walked out with her still-wet hair hanging over her shoulders.

"You're going to be alright with wet hair, yeah?"

She nodded, not really caring about it. "With this heat, it'll probably be dry before we get to the station."

He shrugged, and opened the car door. "I can't argue with that logic," he said, and he climbed in.

Chapter 10

The station was quiet. She frowned as she looked around, following him through the halls. The walls were painted a pale blue. The flooring was laminated, with scuff marks streaking across the ground.

As they finally made it to the front office, they took the first door on the left into the main room where all the desks were scattered across the area.

"Take a seat," he said, pointing towards a low blue seat beside a computer. A small cardboard nameplate was facing her, as she frowned.

"This is cute," she said with a smile. SHe picked it up delicately and showed it to him.

"Yeah," he huffed, not paying much attention to it. He turned to his computer and brought up the file on the investigation to go through the facts again. Then, turned towards Katie.

"All right. So, who did you speak to when you were asking questions?" he asked her.

She shrugged. "I spoke to a lot of people. Including the bartender."

"WHat did he say?"

She smiled. "He said it was a shame about her getting a divorce. Apparently, before this holiday, they had been arguing a lot. She suspected another woman, and her brother-in-law was never happy about them being together in the first place."

"What is she doing here?" a female voice demanded. Katie looked up to see who was speaking about her so harshly, to find a woman wearing a skirt-suit, heavy makeup and red curly hair.

"This is Katie," he stated, as though that was meant to explain everything.

"Right. So what is she doing here?" she asked again, her tone hardening. "This is a precinct, not a support group. Why is she here?"

He sighed, though he kept his tone level with hers. "She's answering questions," he told her, gesturing towards Katie. "The victim was her friend. And she had spoke to a lot of the staff. I am gathering intel on what was said, and when. Then, match them up to what those people told us."

"And why would we believe Katie?" the woman frowned.

"Because," he stated again. "She didn't do it."

"You know that for a fact?"

"Angelia. Trust me on this. I had her look into it. I know what nursery she attended, her favourite teacher, her first pet and first crush. And I checked all the way up to her recent activities, including the drinking binge last month, and the coffee. She's clean."

Katie looked at them, her eyes wide. "You did what now?"

The detective looked back at her with a smirk. "Yes, you heard me, Miss Pinkie."

Katie blushed a deep red.

"You had no right!" she snapped.

"No? You'd rather me keep assuming you're the killer?"

As if that was debatable! She let out a manic laugh. "Yes! If it meant keeping the "Pinkie" out of it, and the nursery stuff - heck yes!"

"Too bad," he replied. "I did my job. Now, I know you're harmless and couldn't possibly have done it."

She glared at him. "Insult me again and I will show you just how harmless I am."

"What are you gonna do? Throw your teddies at me."

Her face grew darker. The humiliation from him gnawed at her nerves, and he was loving it. She tilted her head for a moment. He wants to mess with her, she'll mess with him. And she has a whole book to do it in.

"I will give you three motives for Jenny being dead."

"Motives?" he laughed. "Everyone has a motive. If you want me to be convinced that you are capable of anything, you'll need to do a lot more than that to convince me."

She cleared her throat. If she gets hold of the killer before he does... she shook her head. "You just wait. I am no damn butterfly."

The woman sniggered and stormed off, leaving Katie glaring at her from across the room.

"Who the hell is she?" She demanded. She didn't like her, at all. Not that she understood why, apart from the obvious gutsiness that she carried.

"Angelia is just my colleague. Detective Ann is a good person. We used to be partners."

"Partners?" She liked that idea even worse. "Then if it is past tense, why is she so uptight about me being here?"

He sighed. "Because you're not meant to be," he stated. "I could lose my job if they think I'm giving out evidence."

"You're not giving me anything. I'm just telling you what I know."

He nodded, and leaned in. "Let's keep it that way. At least, until the case is over."

Katie sat across the table from the detective, her heart racing as they discussed the details of the investigation. She couldn't help but feel drawn to him, admiring his sharp mind and dedication to solving the case.

As they delved deeper into the evidence, Katie found herself lost in their words, her eyes lingering on the way their lips moved as they spoke. She couldn't deny the growing attraction she felt towards him, and she wondered if he felt the same, although she doubted it.

Suddenly, the detective looked up from the file they were studying and caught her gaze. Their eyes locked, and for a moment, the air between them crackled with electricity.

Katie's heart skipped a beat as the detective leaned forward, his eyes still fixed on hers. "You seem distracted," he said, his voice low and husky.

Katie swallowed hard, her cheeks flushing. "I—I'm just trying to keep up with all the information," she stammered.

The detective chuckled softly, his eyes sparkling with amusement. "You're doing just fine," he said, a hint of a smile playing at the corners of their lips.

Katie felt her heart race even faster as she realised he was flirting with her. She couldn't wait to see where this investigation would lead them; both, solving the case and in exploring the growing attraction between them.

"Hey!" a voice cut through her stupor. Rather than a hint of warmth coming from him, there was nothing but a hard frown.

Right, she thought, shaking her head. *I almost forgot he's an asshole.*

She had a type. She supposed, she always had. It was why she had often given her characters a bit of an age gap between her characters. The men in her stories, even as a tween, were a few years older than her. And as she grew older, the men in her books matured. Streaks of silver began to appear, and the faces of her characters had grown weathered and worn.

"Did you hear me?" The detective asked.

She blinked, realising that she hadn't been paying attention.

"Yeah," she said, half listening. "You want to talk to the bartender again."

He nodded. "Yes. I want to see if the story he told you matches up with what he tells me. But to do that," he explained, leaning in towards her, "I need you to stay outside."

"Stay outside?!" She gasped. "What am I meant to do whilst you're chatting inside? What if I need a drink?"

He raised an eyebrow. "There is more than one bar in the resort, remember. Go to the poolside bar. You can wait in the pool with a glass of wine until I return."

Wine in the pool? His voice echoed in her mind, as she stared at him in awe. "That is a great idea," she said, truly stunned. "I like how you think."

He frowned, already regretting his decision. "Just... don't get drunk. Too much alcohol on top of this heat would not end well."

That, she thought to herself, *is without a doubt.*

Half an hour passed before they made their way back to the resort. Katie stared out of the window, lost in thought. As she watched the world pass her by, a reflection in a window caught her attention. A small red jacket was draped on the shoulders of a short woman, with nothing on her feet. Walking alongside her, a taller muscular man with a face full of beard, was carrying a pair of red heels under his arm and had a clutch bag hooked on his fingers. She grabbed her own bag and pulled out a notepad and pen, quickly scribbling a few lines of her story. She smiled, admiring what her story was becoming.

Detective James and his partner, Katie, arrived at the Spanish resort just as the sun was beginning to set. The air was warm and the breeze was soft, carrying the scent of saltwater from the nearby beach. They had been sent to the resort to investigate the disappearance of a wealthy businessman, and they were hoping to find some clues that would lead them to him.

As soon as they checked into their room, Katie wasted no time in making herself comfortable. She changed into a bright yellow sundress and headed straight for the poolside bar. Detective James followed her, keeping a watchful eye on the other guests.

Katie ordered a mojito and settled onto a barstool, her eyes scanning the area. She noticed a group of men playing cards at a nearby table, and a couple of women lounging on sunbeds, sipping cocktails. She struck up a conversation with the bartender, hoping to glean some information about the missing businessman.

James watched from a distance, observing the other guests and keeping an eye on Katie. He had worked with Katie for several years, and he knew that she had a knack for gathering information. He trusted her instincts and was confident that she would be able to uncover something that would help them solve the case.

As the night wore on, the poolside bar became more crowded. The music grew louder, and the laughter of the other guests filled the air. Katie ordered another drink and continued to chat with the bartender, keeping her eyes and ears open for any useful information.

James watched as Katie worked, impressed by her skill and dedication. He knew that they still had a long way to go in their investigation, but he had faith that they would be able to solve the case with Katie's help.

As they left the bar and headed back to their room, The Detective turned to Katie and said, "You did a great job tonight. I have a feeling we're going to get to the bottom of this soon." Katie smiled, feeling confident and eager to continue their investigation.

Chapter 11

Katie slumped back after viewing hours of statements, seeing which one matched with what she was told and which ones were different. She highlighted each section and each question. She highlighted keywords that she thought were suspicious before finally giving the detective her findings.

"What's up?" the detective chided, greeting her as he carried two cups of coffee over to the desk.

"You spoke to the bartender yesterday, and on your notes, you mentioned that Jenny was staying with her best friend."

"That's right," he said, nodding.

"Well, he lied." She told him. "She was initially with her husband. But he died shortly after arriving. He only told you that Jenny was staying with a best friend, because that was what I told him. It was my ...excuse, I suppose... that I used to get some answers."

"Ok. So then, that would explain why he said that. Especially if you'd told him otherwise."

Again, she nodded. "Yeah, but he told me she was down because her and the husband hadn't been getting on well. And he mentioned the divorce to me, but we're yet to find the papers."

"So, you're back on the theory that the husband did it?"

Katie shrugged. "It seems that way. If the husband wanted to divorce her, why wait until the holiday to pass her the papers? Why not wait until they got home? Unless..."

The penny dropped. "Unless he wasn't expecting her to survive the holiday to get home in the first place."

It took a while for the discussion to end. Katie stared at him waiting for him to reply. "So? I still don't understand what you're talking about." He said.

"Then you wasn't listening."

"You may have a point," he said.

"He remembered what I told him, and what he was telling me; she was there and then he left. So if he has handed her the divorce papers, where is it?"

"I don't remember seeing some papers when we searched."

"Right," she said, prompted him to explain further. "There was no doubt that he was lying. Which then means that the bartender has something to hide... or the husband took the papers with him; if he did make it back, obviously, it would be likely. But there's no proof that it's close to being finalised."

"So... what if they are on the holiday given the news about knowing it, knowing full well that she won't be alive long enough for it. We need to dig into both of them to find out what their finances would be if she had anything in a will. And find out what the bartender got out of it or her death."

"Really?"

"Yes, really?"

How was she going to find out which one is the real killer? Katie knew she would have to do some digging. How is she going to speak to all three of them without getting them suspicious of what she was doing? She found she knew who she could talk to and she supposed she could try indicating what she thinks. Throw them off her. At least him that way. But they buy it. She wasn't sure. She frowns thinking how else you could approach them under the guise of Alcohol Alcohol is usually a good indicator. Allow them to drop their guard just enough to slip out some information. Of course, it could all horribly backfire. She saw it again and turned towards the bar dozens of people waiting outside showing up to go on. The holiday that was freshly arrived they were the first during the scorching day. She didn't blame them besides the first thing she did, when she arrived, other than unloading her baggage. She strode up to the front flashing the bartender her best smile. "Hello again." She said almost sweetly. "I take it you've been really busy."

The bartender nodded towards the door. "You didn't just walk in, did you?"

"Of course not!" she said. He looked like he didn't believe she had a platinum pass. She didn't have to wait long, though. "You know that's for when you get inside but not for the actual outside the game." "What difference does it make? I'm here because it's not fair to the others. Are you down for speaking about the affair?" She said. "We detectives are watching us, you know."

"Why?"

"Because I know you're lying, of course. Though, the detective isn't convinced." she said, and leaned in to whisper. She looked around watching to see if anyone else was looking for trying to listen in. "The police think the husband did it." She said. He began shaking his head.

"I think it's the husband as well."

"Yeah?"

She sat there, not thinking about it too much.

"I also said "don't get enough divorce." So who knows? Maybe I'm wrong. Maybe the husband did do it. She clearly wasn't happy."

This wasn't news. It was based on wishy washy circumstance. Like he couldn't make his mind up her to believe. There again, she was in the same boat. She wasn't sure.

"You must have seen something, though, right?" she pushed.

The bartender frowned, straightening his posture before taking a cautious step back.

"This is a trap!" he realised, gasping. "You're trapping me into saying something stupid! Are you trying to get me killed?!"

She shook her head defiantly. "No no no, it's not like that!"

The bartender glared at her. "I don't believe you."

He walked away, leaving Katie calling out over the bar. "Hey! What about my drink?!"

He spoke quietly to his colleague, then walked out. The colleague walked towards her, passing her a tall glass. "Take this, then leave," he told her quietly. He was a shorter man, but his stern manner made up for his stature.

"But I didn't do anything," she objected.

The bartender with red hair shook his head. "No matter. You upset him, so, you're leaving,"

With nothing else to say, she downed her drink and slammed the empty glass on the table, hard. Then, stormed out, wondering who else to speak to. A shadowy figure caught her eye, lurking behind a far wall, before disappearing. "Well, fuck," she cussed. Someone knew she'd been asking questions, but who?

Katie walked along the curb of the south side of the resort. The street was unusually quiet. She wondered if the other holiday-goers were already in the pool. She sighed, brushing off her feeling of unease. Perhaps crowds wasn't the best place to hang out, she thought warily. Especially since she didn't know who the shadowed figure was. She looked around again, then hastened her steps towards the quiet pool on the other side of the resort. At least then, she could see anyone approaching. The down side of that, however, also meant that there was only one way out. If the killer found her, there would be no place to run. She glanced at the pool. The still water reflected the clear blue sky above her. The sound of footsteps echoed across the hard concrete. She held her breath, and edged her way towards the water. Can she hold her breath? How long could she hide for? Her heart pounded against her chest, fighting the urge to run. The gate swung open. Fear gripped her, as she struggled to breathe. Without thinking, she grabbed the first thing she could reach. A long plastic pole, meant to hold the closing signpost in the dirt. The bottom end is carved into a curved point.

"What the hell do you think you're doing?!"

A woman's voice cut through the atmosphere like a surgical knife.

Kate watched her, staggering back, stammering. "I-I thought I was being followed," she said, trying to explain.

"Followed? You expect me to believe that?" The woman's tone was cold and hard, with deliberate sarcasm.

"It's true. I was talking to..." she caught herself quick. A thought flashed through her mind. What if this woman was the killer? She just assumed it was one of the men, but could she have been the one to kill Jenny?

"What are you doing here anyway?" Katie frowned. "I'm the only one here. I am sure that you'd be more useful in the busier pool."

The woman snorted and whipped her hair behind her shoulder. "There's a reason no one is in this pool," she chided.

"Why?" Katie demanded, remaining guarded.

The woman pointed to the sign post that Katie was still holding on to. "Read it."

KATIE FROWNED AND TURNED the signpost to the right way up. "Closed for maintenance" she said, reciting the words in bold. "Ooh. My bad."

She glared at her with a hard stare.

"Do you think this is funny?" the woman demanded.

Katie frowned. She had no idea who this woman was, but she certainly wasn't going to be spoken to with such a harsh tone, especially when it was completely unwarranted.

"Funny?" Katie scoffed, holding out her chin. "You mean like how you treated me being chased, so lightly? There is a killer out there, and you think me being chased is amusing."

The woman's hard expression started to waver.

"You were being serious?"

Katie was dumbfounded. Did everyone forget their brains today? "Yes!" she cried out exasperatedly. "I am. And I don't know who it was, but all I know is that someone killed my friend, and I may be next!"

"Have you spoken to the police about this?"

Katie laughed, feeling a little manic. "When have I had the chance to tell them someone had seen me asking questions. You came to me, right after I was chased down, remember? Did you see me speak to the police yet?"

"No, I guess not."

Katie let out a long breath as she tried to regain some of her composure.

Then, she took out her phone and began to dial in the numbers.

Just as the phone began to ring, something hard slammed hard at the back of her head and everything went black.

Chapter 12

Katie came to, with a beautiful setting. A park, she thought, slightly dazed. She could feel the breeze brushing lightly against her skin and the sun's warmth against her face. She groaned, looking around. The clearing was lined with trees, and she could hear the chirping of some birds singing close by.

To her right, another person was tied up to a tree. Her face was battered and bruised with a cut in her bottom lip. Her eyes were red and puffy as though she had been crying, and her neat skirt-suit was torn. She must have put up quite a fight on the way down, she thought proudly. She looked up. The sun was quite high, and the area was largely shaded by the tree branches. She frowned, estimating it to be sometime in the early afternoon. Her stomach grumbled. Perhaps later in the afternoon, she thought, second guessing herself. She was starving. Looking to her left, she could see a small group of men were huddled a few feet away from her.

"Ppst!" Katie whispered, trying to get the woman's attention without alerting the attackers. She frowned, it hadn't occurred to her that there might have been more than one person involved. She thought hard, trying to piece the investigation together. Nothing was making sense. She was sure one of them would be the bartender. She watched as the men disbanded and one of them approached her, their face hidden behind a plastic Halloween mask of a clown; like this was a joke.

"Let me guess," she said, glaring up at them from the ground. Her hands tied behind her, as she leaned back against a large tree.

"The brother in law, right?" she mused.

The man shook his head laughing."No. But I can see why you would think that."

"The husband then," she said, throwing her next suspect out into the open.

He fell silent. "What makes you think I am the husband?"

She smiled. "Because, it is always the husband. So bloody predictable."

"Well then, I'm pleased I didn't disappoint."

She froze. "Not the husband? Really?"

A longer pause. "Or would it be the ex-husband now?"

He sneered at her. "I am not married to her, nor have I ever been."

That left the last person in her suspect list. Her throat was dry. "You're not the husband or the in-laws then. But I'm guessing you're working alongside them in either case. Was it for money?"

"No!" he snapped."Money's no good to me."

She pressed her lips together. Maybe she wasn't completely wrong about her conclusion then. Just who was speaking. She took a deep breath.

"I doubt it has anything to do with love," she commented, looking bored.

"You'd be right on that one. Now, if you don't mind, tell me exactly what you know about that woman's murder."

Katie glared at him. She would've called the police, but she had no doubt that they would have destroyed her phone or left it at the resort.

"You first," she muttered, gritting her teeth.

He leered over her and slammed the back of his hand against her cheek. She cried out, feeling the sudden sting of the slap.

"You hit like a girl!" she taunted.

He snarled at her and struck her again. The impact from the second hit split open her top lip. She cried out in pain. The man in the mask sniggered, and asked her again.

"Now. Tell me. What. Do. You. Know?"

"I know you're a bitch," she retorted. "I know she was poisoned, and I know that she probably has a large fortune on her life insurance. I am guessing, since you claim not to want her money, that the inheritance that you're after is worth a lot more than the money she has. Also, that you were probably the one that supplied the poison. So, it's your turn. Was the murder before or after working in the bar, Mr Bartender."

"How did you know it was me?" he growled, ripping off his mask.

She thought it was ironic, if she would die at his hand. "You were the last name on my suspect list."

"Who else knows?" he demanded, angrily. "Who else knows I am involved in this?!"

She laughed. This asshole had no idea what he had walked into.

"Everyone," she told him defiantly. "Everyone knows. And right now, the police are in your home searching every inch of your property."

He froze, staring at her as though he had tried to read her mind. "You're bluffing," he challenged.

"Am I though?" she said with a smirk of her own.

"Yes. You probably didn't even mention our conversation. Just as I told the police that she was here with you."

"Yes, that was clever," she said, though her tone was unchanged. "Except for the fact that it was me that told you I was here for her. But, by that point, I had already told the police that I just happened to see that she was in trouble and she told me about the fight with her husband. It was you who told me about the divorce." She paused, and then continued. "If you hadn't mentioned the divorce, I wouldn't have suspected you at all. But as soon as you said that he had asked her for a divorce whilst here, and before leaving, I had to think. Why would someone file for a divorce whilst on holiday, unless they know they're not going to make it back to finalise it."

"Hmm..." he muttered thoughtfully to himself. He turned his attention back to her with a smirk. "Too bad that you and your friend here couldn't reach out for help in time."

Katie only laughed. "Really?"

He frowned. "What?"

"Did you speak at all when you attacked us?"

He grew quiet, thinking back. Trying to replay the events leading up to this.

"Uh... I - I don't think so."

"Not even a cough, or cried out when my "friend" fought back on the way down?"

His face paled.

"Yeah," she said with a satisfied hiss. "I had already pushed the call button. So that attack on us was recorded, Bitch."

She smirked at him, holding his gaze.

"What else do they know?"

She shrugged. Although, trying to ignore her body's trembling. "Depends on the question." she said, as if this was a daily routine, and a normal Tuesday.

"The question is," he said again, slowly and deliberately, "What else do they know?"

"Ooh!" She gasped. "Oh, they know lots of stuff. They know that you're not the brains behind the operation. You're not smart enough. They know you have your own motives. They probably know why you've done it. They know where you work and where you live. But the army base doesn't know; if that makes you feel a little better."

She taunted him again. growing confidence by the minute. "They also don't know if you took a shit this morning." She cackled.

He slammed his fist into her face. She held her cheek, trying not to cry out. "You'll pay for that." She growled and passed out again.

Chapter 13

When she came to, the woman beside her looked even more beaten than she had before even more. "Hey!" she said, "what happened?"

"I'll tell you what happened," she groaned. "You got smart and so they knocked you out."

"It's not my fault their idiots," Katie said, shaking her head. "Besides I'm not going to let them get away with this. With any luck the detective will find us, and he'll have backup."

"You can't live in hope," the woman told her. She turned away, seeing hand-prints on the back of her neck. "What did they do to you?" she asked her. "Nothing I can't handle," she replied. "But you need to watch what you're saying."

"Listen," Katie said, and whispered. "I know it's dark right now, but to survive this, we just need to buy ourselves some time; stall them until they get here. We need to keep them talking." she said, continuing her train of thought. "Perhaps we can find out what their end goal is. Then we'll have something to tell The Detectives when they get here. They already have them on kidnapping and assault and murder this could be attempted murder. But we just got to stay alive for now, we can't let them win."

"That's easy for you to say," she retorted.

She shifted uncomfortably, the hard ground beneath her made it difficult to set in one place without having to move around. She could feel the sun beaming on top of her head. Surely someone will find them soon, she thought. Though, she wondered how she was going to get out of this.

"Hey you!" she called out, trying to get the men's attention.

"Oh look who's awake," the bartender replied, snarling. "What do you want?"

"What I have always wanted!" she snapped back. "I want to know why you killed my friend. I want to know what it is that you were trying to inherit, if that's what you want to call it. What's so valuable that you needed her dead?"

He thought for a minute before turning his attention back to her. "What she has," he replied, "is a cabinet. And inside the locked cabinet, in the cosy corner of her room, is a unique ornament that I would like to have. She was not willing to give it to me, however, her husband does want money. But what he doesn't realise is that the item that I want, as you have said so plainly earlier, is worth a lot more than the money that she has."

Katie gasped, disgusted. "You killed her over an ornament?!"

"What can I say?" the bartender replied, in his sing-song kind of voice. "I live for the simple things."

"There is nothing simple about murder," she retorted, "and you will get what's coming to you and will not be getting the ornament that you so desire."

The bartender walked over towards the woman shoved her to one side before making his way back towards Katie. He tied a blindfold around the woman's head, and all Katie could do was watch in horror. The woman couldn't see who had shoved her. "I found a nice little spot for you."

The bartender grabbed the woman by the arm and marched her over to where two holes were dug out; six foot by six inch, deep enough to hide two bodies. "You can't do this!"

"Do... what?" he replied. "We know we'll be found sooner or later. So we'll discard you both now; less baggage to slow us down."

The inside of her ribs ached, her heart pounded against the chest. She looked at her face pale, eyes wide. "Please. I won't tell anyone," the resort attendant pleaded.

The bartender turned towards Katie, then, pulled a blade from his belt. He gave her a quick flash of a smile, then slashed the blade across the woman's neck.

Katie screamed. "No!" Then watched her as she stumbled into the hole face first. She gasped, choking on her hot tears running down her cheeks. She still didn't know her name.

He stepped forward. He sheathed his blade still gleaming from the blood of his previous victim. "You're next," he said.

Katie took a step back. Trying to inch yourself away from the gaping hole. "You can't kill me," she told him. "You just can't!"

"Oh? No? What are you gonna do about it?" he said. Unable to think of retort sufficient enough to scare him away, she lived in hope and said what ever came out of her mouth - hoping it would be something smart. "You kill me..." she said. "It would be a huge mistake. We'd haunt you until your very own grave."

He laughed. "There's no such thing as ghosts."

"You think you there's no such thing as ghosts?" She smirked, and glanced over to the hole where the woman was laying, lifeless and still pooling out with blood, seeping into the soil. "You better hope so," she replied. "Otherwise, my friend, she's going to be visiting you in your dreams and giving you your worth. She will become your worst nightmare." She told him, threatening him and laughed.

Just as he reached out to silence her, red and blue flashing lights surrounded them.

She tried to escape but quickly found herself face down in the dirt.

"Where do you think you're going?" the bartender growled, pulling her up by the hair. "We're not letting you go. You know too much, and you'll probably tell the enforcers our little plan."

Katie laughed, though it hurt her to do so. "Probably is looking a lot more than definitely. And I am going to tell them that you slap like a bitch."

He tried to ignore her, she could tell. She smirked, watching as she got under his skin.

"And to think, I believed you when you told me she had been drinking that day."

Katie watched for his reaction. "Was anything you told me true?" she prompted. She looked around, trying to buy as much time as she could. There had to be a way out of this. There was no chance she was going to end up in a hole somewhere. She turned her head slightly, eyeing the garbage bag in the corner that was meant to hide her body. Was they going to even dispose of her properly? She groaned inwardly in disgust. What would her mother think? She would roll her eyes and talk to her friends about how typical it was that she would wind up in a ditch. The fact that she might even be right, riled her up. She growled to herself, trying to think of any other way for her to survive this. But one thing was for sure, there was no way she was going to let the killers get away with the murders they committed. One murder was bad enough, but killing the hotel staff as well? Not to mention her own life on the line, well, enough was enough .She shook her head defiantly, bringing herself enough courage to stand on her feet. Her legs felt weak beneath her. Pained from the abrasions from being on the ground, she used a near by tree to steady herself.

"What now?" the bartender demanded.

"I want to choose my own death," she voiced.

The bartender looked at her as though she had just spat out something so incomprehensible, that he wasn't sure it was even in the same language.

"What?" he asked, raising an eyebrow.

"You heard me. If I am to die, I want to choose my own death."

"Why would I allow that?"

"Because the results will still end up the same way. I will be dead, and you would have maybe a week before you're arrested and named as a serial killer, whilst your buddies get away scott free without any consequences on their part."

"What do you mean scott free? What are you talking about? None of us are going to prison."

Katie laughed, slightly tilting her head. "It's so cute that you think they would stay by you. But the moment the cops ask them questions, they will pin everything on you. Why do you think they are so eager to keep you at a distance? Did you notice that they keep disappearing and running errands?"

He fell silent as he pondered her words. She kept talking. "It is to maintain an alibis. Then they have some circumstantial evidence that they hadn't done anything. Whereas, you, have not been in front of a camera one single time, alone or without me. You are their scapegoat. And I am pretty sure they have no intention of giving you that ornament that you want so bad."

"You don't know what you are talking about."

She fell silent, letting the words sink in, just for a moment. Then she shrugged casually, as though she dismissed the whole thing. "You're probably right. I mean, you know them really well, right? Test them. Ask them to watch me whilst you run an errand of your own. I bet you my life that they will make excuses for you not to be out of my sight."

He looked out towards the bushes, where the truck is parked silently on the side of the road. It seemed to be abandoned once again.

"They've been taking an awful long time to get something to drink," she remarked.

His eye twitched. Her words had been sinking in, and she was getting through to him. Now, all she had to do was unravel the rest of his confidence in them and pull them apart. She smiled to herself. By the end of this trip, not only will he hand himself in, but he'll take down the others too, simply out of spite.

He hauled her away from the tree and shoved her into the back of the van. She grunted, feeling the hard cold metal beneath her skin.

"Where are we going now?" she demanded.

He looked at her for a moment before speaking. "If they're going to make sure I am getting caught, I'm not about to hang about. We're leaving again, and they can fend for themselves. In the meantime, I am sure I can find a nice and quiet spot to bury you in. And you can pick your cause of death. You can be stabbed, shot or you can drown. Either way, it really doesn't concern me." he paused briefly before echoing her own words back to her. "It's the same result. Right?"

She cleared her throat. It wasn't quite what she had in mind. She thought for a minute, growing frantic as the van doors slammed closed and engulfing her in darkness. Only a slither of light made its way through the gaps in the hinges of the door. She closed her eyes, trying to keep calm. It was a van. It was like tin. She frowned, looking around. There was nothing inside that she could use to grab anyone's attention. Then she looked down at her feet. She sighed. The only thing left to do when things weren't going her way. She turned towards one of the sides of the van and kicked as hard as she could.

One of two things were going to happen. Maybe three, if she was being realistic. She'll either make so much noise on the road that someone will hear and come to rescue her. Or, she will kick the damn door open, and everyone will see she is in trouble and call the authorities. Or, something she deemed a lot more likely. No one else will notice the noise she was making, and the bartender will be driven nuts by the constant banging that he would have no choice but to deal with. That too, carried some risk. Either, it would result in hastening her death, or he will open the door long enough for someone else to come and help her. She hoped the authorities would arrive in a hurry, but given the circumstances... she only hoped he would be distracted long enough for her to escape and find help herself. She frowned. So many risks. She wasn't even sure it would be worth it.

She slammed her feet hard against the side, stamping as much as she could. If she could escape.... And stay alive.

Chapter 14

Kate continued to slam her feet against the side of the van. It stung her soles, but she didn't care. If it would get someone's attention, it would be more than worth it.

"Stop that banging!" a voice screamed from the front. The bartender's voice barely cut through the sound of the traffic and the van's engine.

"What's the matter?" she taunted. "Worried someone will hear me?"

He continued to drive, saying nothing more.

She went back to kicking the back of the van, now slamming her feet against the back door. Gradually, the door began to give way to her. She smiled, and kicked harder.

Of course, it didn't take him long to realise what she was doing and began to pull over. She couldn't see where they were, but she felt the pull of the van as it slowed to a stop. She could feel the uneven ground as they drove over grass on the side. She held her breath, hoping that someone was driving behind them and seeing what was going on. Though, she knew it wasn't likely. He wasn't that stupid.

"Hey!" he shouted again, bursting the back doors open. "I told you to cut it out!"

She shrunk back and bit her lip. They were alone. But it wasn't all lost. It didn't take her long to recognise where they were.

"I'm sorry," she said, looking around casually. "Who was I bothering?"

He was about to answer when she turned and glanced at the make and model of the van. It was the first time she had managed to get a good look at it without being rushed into the back, It wasn't as old as she was expecting it to be. It was in fairly good condition, and going by the licence plate, it was less than five years old.

She smirked. She didn't know a lot about vans or cars, but there was one thing she was certain of.

"Hey," she said, smirking at him.

"What now?"

"So... what are you planning to do when you get caught?" she asked.

"I told you, I won't. You'll die, and that'll be the end of it."

She laughed to herself. It was only a matter of time before the police cotton on and save her. The path was fairly straight forward. She remembered passing it on the way to the hotel. It seemed almost a lifetime ago. How long has it been? Two weeks? She was desperate to go home. Her writing had suffered, she hadn't written since the mess began. She thought back to her new friend. What would she have done? She supposed it wasn't a hard question. She knew. She took a deep breath, preparing herself for her fight of survival. Then, when he turned to face the van with a confused look on his face, she bolted across the field.

She was fast, but he was faster. Kate ran until her heart pounded against her chest. She could hear his footsteps catching up with her, but she didn't dare look behind her. She could almost imagine his breath on the back of her neck. Run, she thought, screaming at herself. *Run faster. Run harder. Stay alive.*

Suddenly, she was shoved from behind. A large weight thrust onto her, tackling her to the floor.

"You're gonna die for this," he growled, hauling her from the ground by the collar of her shirt.

"I'm gonna die anyway, ain't I? Who ever said I was gonna make it easy for you?"

She never liked running. She wished she wore her heels, at least then she would have some sort of weapon. She frowned. There had been other fights in the past. Not all of them were weaponised. She cleared her throat, and watched him. "You're gonna be so sorry though," she said, forewarning him.

"Yeah? Who's gonna stop me?"

"I am."

He laughed. He laughed harder than she thought he had ever laughed in his life. "You? What can you do? You're helpless."

She pressed her lips together. *Helpless*. She hadn't drank coffee for more than a week. She wouldn't exactly say she was helpless. She took a deep breath, raised her hands slowly, and then whilst he was distracted by her hands, she swiftly kicked him in the kneecap.

He yelped, letting her go as he crumbled to the floor. She kicked him again, but he blocked her.

He took out his blade from his pocket, pointing it towards her.

"This is as good as any place to die anyway," he snapped.

He launched towards her. She wasn't fast enough, catching the blade's edge across her arm. She yelped out in pain, feeling the blood warm her skin. She glanced down at it.

"You bastard," she growled. She moved quicker, she drove towards him, tackling him to the ground. She threw her fists at his face, flailing her arms trying to make contact at least half the time. He covered his face, blocking her attack. She paused, and waited. She watched as he slowly lowered his arms from his face, then, using her fingernails in the only way she knew. She shoved him straight into his eyes.

He screamed, throwing her off him. She flew off, feeling her back slam into a nearby tree. She groaned, trying to get to her feet.

"Fuck it!" he cussed, and reached around to his other pocket. "I have been patient enough. But no. Now I have to end this."

He pulled out a gun.

Her eyes widened. He had a gun the whole time?

"Are you kidding me?" she gasped, her eyes transfixed on the barrel.

"I don't like using guns," he confessed. "It's too loud. It'll give away our location. But I think we're at a distance enough to make an exception. Any last words?"

She took a deep breath again. "You know what new vans have, what old vans dont?" she asked.

"What?" he growled, though his tone had a hint of uncertainty.

"GPS tracking devices," she said, and grinned.

Sirens blared in the background. She didn't move. He still held the gun towards her.

"They come near me, I'll shoot," he growled.

Kate rolled her eyes. "And then, they'll shoot you. And I have been making sure I have a spot in hell - and I'll be making sure I'm the one torturing you for all eternity."

He raised his gun. His finger resting on the trigger.

"Freeze!"

Epilogue

He pulled the trigger. Kate threw herself onto the ground. Feeling the straw like texture against her skin. She cried out in pain. She didn't move fast enough. Another bang. The detective fired off a shot, putting a bullet square into the bartender's shoulder.

"I am not going to kill you," the detective screamed, as he went to Katie's aid. "I want to make sure you pay for what you have done."

He turned towards her with a softened smile. "Are you all right?"

She shook her head. "No. Bastard shot me. I really want to shoot him back."

"It's not worth it," he told her. He ordered his men to take him, and then helped Katie into the back of his car and drove to the nearest hospital.

She was there for almost a week. Her plane back home was long gone and her story was no closer to being finished. She had thought long and hard about what her next story would be.

She smiled, thinking about her friend, Jenny. She didn't have to die. She opened her laptop that the detective had dropped off for her and watched the cursor blink on the screen. Perhaps she didn't need to die completely. She reread the opening sentences of her new story.

"How dare you?!" she screamed, turning red in the face as she faced her husband. His pants still strawn across the bedroom floor. Beside him, in her bed, was her best friend.

Yes, Jenny was going to have a lot of adventures.

Just then the detective walked in.

"You're awake!" He cheered. He leaned down and planted a kiss on her forehead. "I have some news. The husband and the brother have been apprehended. And you have two weeks added to your holiday, free of charge."

She smiled at him. "Thanks." She said sweetly.

"What are you gonna do with your time here?"

She didn't need to think about it.

"Oh you know. Sightseeing, eating some food and writing a new story. Want to join me?"

"Heck yeah!" He replied. "I am never leaving your side."

To be continued in...

Book 2 of *A Holiday Mystery*
Dead in Turkey

Did you enjoy this book?

Thank you for reading my book. I hope you enjoyed reading as much as I had enjoyed writing it.

Could you spare a few seconds of your time to write a review? Not only would this let me know what I did right, but also what I could improve on in the next book.

<u>Review this book</u>[1]

---

1. https://www.amazon.com/review/create-review/B0C47D1SY6

About the Author

Michelle Mackenzie is the writer and author of the published novels, The Storm Within, (book 1 of The Dark Queen series). Encouraged by the success of her books, she is continuing her career as a mystery and thriller writer.

About the Publisher

Reflective Line Publishing was launched in August of 2021. Though the company is based in the UK, the founder isn't stopping there, with plans to become a global company and become one—if not the biggest—publishing company.

If you enjoyed reading this book, and would like to keep up-to-date on new books available, subscribe to our mailing list using the link below. You can also find more information about the company on our website.

Website: www.reflectivelinepublishing.wordpress.com[1]

---

1. http://www.reflectivelinepublishing.wordpress.com

Don't miss out!

Visit the website below and you can sign up to receive emails whenever Michelle Mackenzie publishes a new book. There's no charge and no obligation.

https://books2read.com/r/B-A-ZDIQ-BLSIC

BOOKS 2 READ

Connecting independent readers to independent writers.

Milton Keynes UK
Ingram Content Group UK Ltd.
UKHW020845271023
431440UK00015B/497